To my
precious Little
grand child who
I already love so much.
I know your Daddy will
love reading you this book.
Maybe one day you will be
a Derbie fan Like your Daddy
and I. I can't wait for you to
get here.

I love you,
Nana
12-03-05

Hello Aubie!

Aimee Aryal

Illustrated by Danny Moore
Auburn University, Class of 2003

MASCOT BOOKS™

www.mascotbooks.com

It was a beautiful fall day at
Auburn University.

Aubie was on his way to Jordan-Hare
Stadium to watch a football game.

He stopped in front of Hargis Hall.

A professor walking by said,
"Hello Aubie!"

Aubie walked past Samford Hall.

The President of Auburn University
waved, "Hello Aubie!"

Aubie walked over to the
University Chapel.

A couple coming out of
the chapel said, "Hello Aubie!"

Aubie passed by the
Foy Student Union.

A group of students yelled,
"Hello Aubie!"

It was almost time for the football game.
As Aubie walked to the stadium,
he passed by some alumni.

The alumni remembered Aubie from
when they went to Auburn University.
They said, "Hello, again, Aubie!"

Finally, Aubie arrived at
Jordan-Hare Stadium.

He ran onto the football field as Tiger, Auburn's golden eagle, flew around the stadium. Aubie cheered, "War Eagle!"

Aubie watched the game from
the sidelines and cheered for the team.

The Tigers scored six points!
The quarterback shouted,
"Touchdown Aubie!"

At half-time the Auburn University
Marching Band performed on the field.

Aubie and the crowd sang,
"Glory to Ole Auburn."

The Auburn Tigers
won the football game!

Aubie gave Coach Tuberville
a high-five. The coach said,
"Great game Aubie!"

After the football game, Aubie was tired.
It had been a long day at
Auburn University.

He walked home and climbed into bed.

"Goodnight Aubie."

For Anna and Maya, and all of
Aubie's little fans. ~ AA

This one is for my fellow Auburnites.
You guys fuel the fire, baby! War Eagle! ~ DM

Special thanks to:

Susan Smith

Tommy Tuberville

For information please contact Mascot Books,
P.O. Box 220157, Chantilly, VA 20153-0157.

ISBN: 0-9743442-8-1

Printed in the United States.

www.mascotbooks.com